About the Author

After a very adventurous younger life, Diana Sare has settled down to divide her time into summers in the wilds of Canada and winters in a remote area of Panama. Along with her husband Robin, she still manages to travel extensively while painting, keeping up large gardens and spending as much time as possible with the young people in her family.

RANDY
THE RUNAWAY RACCOON

Written and Illustrated By
DIANA SARE

AUSTIN MACAULEY PUBLISHERS™
LONDON * CAMBRIDGE * NEW YORK * SHARJAH

Copyright © Diana Sare (2018)

A CIP catalogue record for this title is available from the British Library.

ISBN 9781528906159 (Paperback)
ISBN 9781528906166 (Hardback)
ISBN 9781528906173 (E-Book)
www.austinmacauley.com

First Published (2018)
Austin Macauley Publishers ™ Ltd
25 Canada Square
Canary Wharf
London
E14 5LQ

Dedication

All the young people in my family.

Contents

A LITTLE RACCOON WAS CROUCHED IN
THE MIDDLE OF ALL THE TRASH

RANDY RACCOON

BANG!   *CRASH!*

As the lid of an old tin garbage can bounced down a dark back lane and clattered to a stop, the can fell off the deck and dumped all its contents onto the lawn.

In the house, an upstairs window was flung open and an old lady with fuzzy white hair looked down at the mess in her yard. She picked up her glasses from the table beside her, but then dropped them as a horrible smell suddenly filled her room. When she got her glasses on, she saw what had happened. A little raccoon was crouched in the middle of all the stinking trash with an empty can in his little black paws and a fish bone hanging from his shoulder.

"Get out of here you nuisance," she yelled, slamming the window shut.

The little raccoon whose name was Randy, looked at her very carefully, wondering if she would come outside or whether he would have time to look for something to eat.

Oh look—half a bag of spotty apples! Now that WAS a find, and worth the worry of staying a little longer. By the time he had finished eating all the apples, including the cores and any worms there might have been, he was feeling a lot better and waddled off down the lane.

After a while, he came to some railroad tracks, and finding a thin trail of grain down the middle, he followed it.

It was a lovely night. There were stars overhead and bright lights in the distance, and having a full tummy made Randy happy and ready to explore.

But as he trotted along, the train tracks seemed to be multiplying and were everywhere. The grain was gone and replaced by blobs of oil. He hadn't been paying attention and now everything was different. Off to the sides where the last he had noticed were grass, weeds and houses, now big buildings rose around him.

Suddenly, a terrible monster was rushing straight towards him! He froze.

Before he could think or move, it roared past him with a horrible howl, and a blast of wind that almost blew him away. It was a train arriving into the city, but Randy had no idea what it was and was so frightened that he peed right down his leg. Then he ran.

He wanted to hide from that awful 'thing', so when he saw a ramp leading up into a shed on a side track, he ran up and dove in. The big shed was full of brand new cars and as he tried to hide, he bumped his nose, and then he...stopped!

Right in front of him he saw a raccoon, although it didn't smell like one. Randy, knowing that he should be polite, said "hello", but though it looked like it was speaking, there was no sound. No smell and no sound meant only one thing to Randy. It must be a ghost!

Shivering with fright, he noticed that the ghost looked just the same. Could ghosts get scared too?

When he moved, it moved in the same direction but seemed to be stuck inside the car. Randy didn't know that he had been seeing his own reflection.

HE SAW A RAMP LEADING UP INTO
A SHED ON A SIDE TRACK

He was tired, confused and worried, but at the same time he was a little bit proud of himself. He'd found lots of food, gone exploring farther than he'd ever heard of before, managed to outwit a HUGE monster and now he was frightening a ghost!

With these reassuring thoughts, he lay down to relax when...SLAM! His shed jerked violently and then started to move! He scrambled to run back down the ramp, but instead, came to another wall. There was no way out!

Through holes in the walls, he saw buildings and trees whizzing by. Then he heard the same long howl that had frightened him so much before and with a horrible feeling in his stomach, he realized that he had accidently gotten inside a 'monster'. His heart thudded so hard it was almost as loud as the wheels on the track. He crouched by the tires of a car feeling sick with fear and smelling quite stinky.

The train rocked back and forth as it made its way out of the city, and after a while, Randy was so worn out by all that had happened, he fell asleep.

He started dreaming about being in a tree that a ghost was shaking. The branches and leaves bashed about wildly, and there must have been a storm because every now and then, there was a crash like thunder or lightning. Then the shaking stopped so that the ghost could have a nice long drink of water. Since they had been playing together all day long in his dream, Randy knew that the ghost was his friend.

A BRIGHT LIGHT SHONE RIGHT INTO HIS EYES

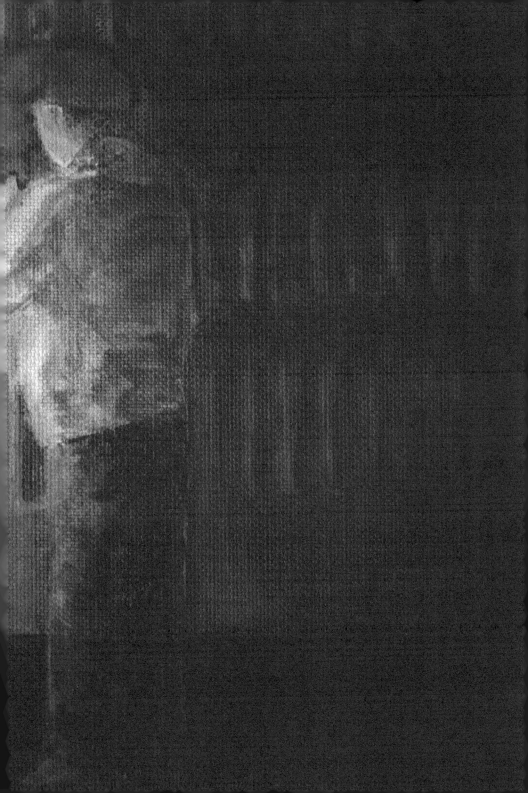

R.R. IS SHORT FOR RAILROAD

Randy jolted awake to the loud squeal of wheels against the metal of the track as the train slowed.

It was night again, and although he was refreshed from his sleep, he was very thirsty.

With a lurch, the train came to a complete stop and all that could be heard was a ticking noise and a quiet whimpering.

Then there was the sound of loud footsteps crunching in gravel and Randy could see a light swinging from side to side as it moved along the train towards him.

"So, what have we here? A runaway?" the deep voice of a night watchman asked.

A bright light suddenly shone right into Randy's eyes, and for a moment, he was completely blinded. "Oh ho! A runaway coon is more like it," the man said. Randy was relieved when the man walked away.

He was so thirsty! If only, he could figure out a way to get out of this cage. Now that he was thinking about water, he could smell it and it seemed to be close.

Soon he heard footsteps returning and saw the light bobbing towards him again. Randy crouched down as close to the inside of a car tire as he could squeeze, hoping that the man would walk by. But no, the man stopped right beside him, shining the light around until he spotted the end of Randy's tail. Then quite quietly, he said, "It's your lucky night runaway. We're stopped for a while so I'm going to let you out."

IT WAS THE MOST BEAUTIFUL SIGHT HE HAD EVER SEEN

With a loud groan, one half of the metal wall opened outward and there in front of him was an escape route.

The only problem was that there was no ramp to leave by. Randy could see that there was quite a drop to the ground and the man was standing nearby, so, would he be able to get away? Or would the man catch him?

He gathered himself together and with a running leap, threw himself over the edge. Landing as a ball of fur, he rolled up onto his four little feet and ran as fast as he could in case the train was after him!

When he paused for breath, there was nothing behind him, just a bad smell which seemed to be coming from himself.

Looking around anxiously, he saw the most beautiful sight he had ever seen. Spread out in front of him was a lake, sparkling in the light of the moon, almost as though the moon was making a pathway for him to walk across.

That was the water he had smelled—the lake. To his left was a row of houses with lights twinkling in the night. To his right was a jagged skyline of evergreen trees that looked like safety.

Randy headed straight into the lake. It was very cold, but so refreshing! After washing his face and paws (his mother had told him "ALWAYS wash your face and hands first"), he combed out his fur, washed his face and paws again in case there was anything stuck there and then drank and drank.

When he had drunk all he could, and felt that he was rid of all the bad smells, he headed off in the direction of the fir trees.

AFTER WASHING ONE VERY CAREFULLY, HE ATE IT

Among bulrushes at the shoreline, he found some crayfish. He didn't know what they were, having never seen one before, but being so hungry, after washing one very carefully he ate it. WOW! It was so fresh, sweet and crunchy, that immediately he decided they were his very favourite food—ever!

Then he dug up some bulrush shoots, planning to clean his teeth, and tried them—very tasty! This place was turning out to be great. There was wonderful food and water and nobody pushing or shoving him, trying to share like back at his nest.

That thought made him stop to think. It was unlikely that he would see his family again after what had happened to him, but he was old enough now to be on his own.

Gazing out over the lake, he felt very happy. Moon light sparkled off little wavelets, stars winked in the night sky, the evergreen trees gave off a strong clean smell, and there was nothing he could see to bother him. A little breeze ruffled his fur and made a soft sighing sound in the trees as he made his way down toward the end of the lake.

A HUGE BLACK FORM EMERGED FROM THE FOREST

Just then, a sharp snapping of twigs made him stop.

He couldn't see or smell anything dangerous, but slowly a huge black form emerged from the forest. It had a really big nose, a sort of bag like thing hanging under its chin, a hump on its back and the biggest antlers imaginable.

After a couple of minutes, and not knowing that he was seeing a moose, Randy thought perhaps it was one of

Santa's reindeer. After all, he was so far from home that he could be at the North Pole by now.

Totally amazed Randy wandered on, downhill mostly, following first this trail and then that, finding ripe little strawberries, and with the smell of water all around him.

HE WRAPPED HIS TAIL OVER HIS EYES AND FELL ASLEEP

As it started to grow light, he found himself in a little clearing beside a pond.

A lot of trees had fallen and one of them had a hole under it, just big enough for a tired raccoon worn out from a hard journey and a busy night.

He caught a few minnows and had a drink from the pond, then crawling as far under the log as he could, wrapped his tail over his eyes and immediately fell into an exhausted sleep.

ACROSS A CLEARING WAS A HUGE LAKE

R.R. IS A RURAL ROUTE ADDRESS

Randy woke up feeling very warm, with the sun shining right on him, and found that he had slept all morning.

Across a clearing, he could see a huge lake with many kinds of birds—squabbling in the water, flying and circling overhead, flitting in and out of the trees and grazing noisily on the land.

Looking around, he found himself in a large open area with several buildings.

Not far from shore, a small sailboat tugged at its anchor as four small otters pretended it was a trampoline; bouncing on the deck and then diving off into the water.

Sometimes, one of them would sneak up underneath and give a sharp poke with its nose, sending the others flying into the lake. They were having so much fun that Randy wanted to join them, but before he could, they swam away.

Going to look around one of the larger buildings, he found a lot of flowers and a nice little patio for sitting and sunning on, and just as he was about to turn away, he spotted a hole which led under the building.

HE SPOTTED A HOLE LEADING UNDER THE BUILDING

Just then, a car drove down and stopped in a cloud of dust. Two people got out and entered a building with some bags of groceries.

Instinct told Randy to hide, so without thinking, he pushed his way into the hole and found that it opened into a spacious cavern under the floor of the building. What a cool and lovely place this would be for a home, he thought.

He was used to people, having lived in a city his whole life, so they were probably okay, unless they had a dog.

There was no sign that anyone else lived here and no smell of a dog around, so with all the food and water, it might be a perfect spot. There was a very faint smell of skunk, but he was much bigger than a skunk and knew that if he could get rid of a monster and a ghost, a skunk would never bother him!

And so, Randy settled into his new home.

He often saw Gramma and Poppa, the people who lived in the house, but they paid no attention to him.

There were lots of other animals, mostly smaller ones like squirrels and chipmunks, but a porcupine told him that there were predators in the area as well.

Randy knew that one of the best ways to be safe from his predators was to live near humans.

THE PLANTS WERE ALL BROKEN AND THE FLOWERS GONE

The first mistake Randy made, was eating the flowers which grew beside the patio right outside his front door.

One day, when Gramma came out to the garden, she noticed that the plants were all broken, and the flowers gone.

She was not happy! And because of the mess he had made of the delphiniums, Gramma decided to get rid of him.

His second mistake was being nosy.

Although naturally cautious, Randy was very curious about anything new, so when Poppa put out a trap with some fruit and vegetables in it, he let it sit there for a while watching the food inside. The trap was an old one which hadn't been used for many years, and when Randy went in it the first time, nothing happened, except he enjoyed eating the treats.

Sometimes either Gramma or Poppa would come and play with the trap, but nothing changed.

One morning, after Randy had had a busy night and was thinking of having a sleep, he entered the trap as usual, but the door slammed shut behind him and he couldn't get out!

TRAPPED!

Randy didn't think that Poppa or Gramma would hurt him (they even offered him more broccoli and celery), but he was so worried, nervous and ashamed, that he peed in the cage. Poppa mopped up as well as he could, picked up the cage, put it in his car and drove off up the road. They went past the store and campground at the little lake that Randy had seen when he first arrived. Then, after turning down a gravel road, Poppa stopped the car, set the cage on the ground and opened the door. Randy just sat quietly hoping for the best, but Poppa started talking and told him that he was free to go. Go? Where?

Randy didn't want to go anywhere. Poppa told him that he shouldn't return to the garden, or have eaten the flowers there. Randy thought that this was more than just greedy. It was rude! There was a lot of food and he'd even been given more every day in the cage. No one else had been eating the flowers, so what were they there for anyway? Just to look pretty?

POPPA SAID TO GET GOING

However, Poppa said to get going and find himself somewhere new. So, after a while, Randy stumbled out of the cage and entered the long grass beside the road.

He wandered into the shade of the trees, where it was cooler and he could think more clearly. Was Poppa wrong?

Did Gramma really care if he ate the flowers? She had given him food. It might not have been crayfish, but it was healthy enough and his mother had always said not to be picky when you were given food.

He wondered—*could he find his way back to the garden?*

CURLED INTO A LITTLE BALL BY THE
TRUNK OF A LARGE RED PINE TREE

All this thinking was making him tired, and as he was used to being up at night and sleeping during the day, his head began to droop. He curled himself up into a little ball, close to the trunk of a large red pine tree and soon was fast asleep. The afternoon passed, the sun slipped to the horizon and then, suddenly was gone, and a gentle breeze wafted through the trees.

When Randy awoke hungry, he set off to find something to eat. Raspberries were starting to ripen by the side of the road and although they were a bit gritty from dust, he ate them anyway. As he got nearer to a farm, a delicious aroma reached his nose. It was a chicken house with eggs.

He wasn't used to chickens, but he sure liked eggs! Slowly, he made his way towards the hen house while keeping an eye out for any dogs. However, this evening the farm dog was asleep inside the house, so it didn't know that Randy was there looking for food.

When he reached the henhouse, Randy climbed up the ramp and carefully unhooked the door, which the farmer had closed for the night. Inside, he disturbed the sleeping chickens as he picked the eggs from under their warm bodies.

LEAVING A MESS OF EGGSHELLS BEHIND AND
THE DOOR WIDE OPEN, HE LEFT

ROSIE AND RHONDA

Crunching down fresh eggs was like a birthday party but better, because all the eggs were for him! He feasted until he was stuffed, and then, leaving a mess of eggshells behind and the door wide open, he left the farm and waddled back down the road.

After a while, he could hear a car coming towards him and soon its lights reflected from his eyes. He slipped off the road, crawled under a barbed wire fence and found himself entering a big hayfield. The hay had been cut and most of it was already baled into great round wheels. It looked like a good place to find small rodents which, had he not been totally full, he liked to hunt.

He snuffled his way happily around the bales, enjoying the smell of the fresh cut hay, when suddenly, he heard a ruckus by the fence. There was shrieking, a thump and the sound of tussling in the grass. Randy wasn't sure if it

would be wise to go and see what was happening. It could be a predator killing something, which would be very dangerous, or it could be someone just fooling around. It didn't smell like trouble and in fact, the smell was quite attractive! Suddenly, something came tumbling out of the long grass, and as he turned an anxious face towards it, he saw that it was a girl raccoon! Almost instantly, another girl's face peeked out nearer still. Then there was silence—except for the whirr of wings passing in the night.

HE INTRODUCED HIMSELF

Randy pulled himself together, plastered a smile across his face and introduced himself in what he thought was a mature and pleasant voice. The girls replied that their names were Rosie and Rhonda and that they were twins from the next farm over. Soon, they were all chattering at the same time, telling each other all about themselves.

Randy regaled them with the story of how he had arrived by train, but didn't mention how frightened he had been. And when he described the beautiful lake, they told him that they knew it well and that it wasn't far away.

They could go there any time they liked, in fact.

Randy asked, very politely, if they were hungry, but when he told them about the hen house, they said no, they weren't, and besides, the dog on that farm was extremely dangerous.

He asked if they knew Gramma and Poppa, but they told him that there were a lot of very dangerous animals in the woods between here and there, so they didn't go in that direction.

When Randy told them about what he had seen and done down by the big lake and how beautiful it was there, they didn't seem very interested. They did say though, that he was very brave for having travelled so far.

They spent a very happy night playing hide and seek among the bales of hay, until the first light started to glimmer in the east. Then, tired out from all their frolicking, they looked for a good spot to sleep. Randy was so very happy to have found friends of his own kind and there was such a wonderful freedom here in the country, that he knew he was just where he wanted to be and that he would never want to return to city life.

THEY PLAYED HIDE AND SEEK AMONG THE BALES OF HAY

RUNNING RAGGED

No sooner had the three friends snuggled all together into a warm little bundle of furs beside a fence post, than they were frightened wide awake by the mad barking of a dog. Rosie and Rhonda jumped up, and ran as fast as they could out onto the road, heading for the ditch on the far side and the safety of trees for them to climb. Wide eyed, Randy was right behind them.

Raccoons are not fast runners and the dog, barking furiously, was gaining on them quickly. The three friends were very tired by the excitement of meeting and the long night of playing, but the dog, who had spent the night sleeping indoors, was feeling invigorated by the cool morning air and the chance to run.

Just as it was crossing the road, Randy, Rosie and Rhonda reached the trees and with desperate gasps, flung themselves up into the safety of the branches. They were in two trees and the dog was jumping and barking below them, trying to catch their tails, or at least some fur. The tree that Randy was in, was big and old with several broken branches. The one in which Rosie and Rhonda were hanging, was young and much smaller. It bent with the weight of the two raccoons when they tried to climb, and wasn't going to be a good place to stay out of reach for long.

THE DOG WAS JUMPING AND BARKING BELOW THEM

Randy was worried about his friends. It didn't look like the dog would leave any time soon, and the girls wouldn't be able to sleep in that little tree. Randy tried to think of some way they could get to his tree before they fell out of the small one they were in. He moved down a bit, which brought the dog over instantly. Then he climbed back up, and the dog went back after the girls. When he went up higher and to the far side, out of sight of the dog, he found something very exciting. There was a big hole in the tree, probably made at first by woodpeckers, and later

perhaps enlarged for a squirrel's nest. It was dry, roomy and filled with dead leaves, twigs, cones and cobwebs. It would be a perfect place to sleep, if he could get the girls over here.

Back at the other side of the tree, the noise was terrible. Randy saw that Rhonda was slipping down a branch and close to falling into the snapping jaws of the frantic dog.

HE FELT SHARP TEETH SINKING INTO HIS BACK LEG

Yelling to the girls, he dropped to the ground. The dog was not about to be distracted from catching Rhonda, so he didn't notice that Randy was right behind him, until he felt sharp teeth sinking into his back leg. Furious, he whipped around to catch Randy, but just as he turned away from her, Rhonda fell from the branch and landed on the dog's back, digging in her claws. The sting of her nails made the dog snap his head back, just in time to be scratched across the nose by Rosie, who had reached the ground.

Randy jumped sideways across the dog, trying to bite it on the side of its neck, giving the girls time to get away. But before he landed, he felt a nasty pain at the end of his tail. From the safety of the big tree which they had reached, the girls screamed at the dog who had Randy's tail in his teeth and was pulling as hard as it could.

THEY THREW DOWN BITS OF TWIGS AND CONES

Randy dug into the ground with his claws and lunged with all his might for the tree, at the same time as the dog opened his mouth to grab Randy's body. The raccoon tore free and in one huge leap, made it to the tree, somersaulted around the trunk, and scrambled as fast as he could up to safety in the branches.

The dog was left with some fur hanging from his mouth as the two female raccoons scolded him from above and threw down bits of twigs and cones.

Randy examined his tail, which was now square across the end and sore from the dog's teeth. There was some blood on his last tail ring and he hoped that the fur would grow back. But if it didn't—well, they were all safe!

And, they had found a fantastic place to stay.

NESTLED TOGETHER LIKE A FAMILY

Together they climbed into the hollow of the tree, shuffled around in the leaves to settle themselves, and then, just as the sun was peeking in on them, fell soundly and securely fast asleep.

The dog, knowing that now there was no hope of catching a raccoon, trotted off for home, lifting his nose in the morning air, searching for the smell of anything interesting that might be around, and proud of himself for having chased the raccoons away from his farm.

HER FUR SHONE WITH LIGHT FROM THE SETTING SUN

REST AND RELAXATION

The three little raccoons were so tired from playing, fighting and fright, that they slept for a long time that day—much longer than usual—and so it was almost dark when they finally awoke. What a comfy sleep they had had!

High up in a tree, nestled into the dry leafy space and all together like a family, they felt safe and content. A big branch to the right of the entrance, was a lovely spot to watch the sun set, but they were hungry and wanted to find a toilet, so they didn't spend any time there then.

When they had all reached the ground, a bit anxious in case the dog might be nearby still, they were very quiet and listened as hard as they could. There were little rustling noises of small animals in the underbrush, and Rosie even thought that she smelled a deer nearby, but nothing frightening. And then they heard wonderful sounds. FROGS SINGING! That meant food and water was near by.

After the girls found an old latrine, they followed the songs of the singing frogs and soon found themselves at the shore of a small lake, whose edges were rocky and reedy. What an evening feast they had!

There were crayfish, mussels, frogs, minnows and lots of fresh water to drink. The hazel nuts were coming ripe, and across the lake Randy could see a pasture with apple trees on another farm.

Randy looked at Rosie. Her eyes were bright and sparkling, and her fur shone with light from the setting sun.

It was golden! Randy felt ecstatic! When Rosie turned her head and looked at Randy, his tummy tingled in surprise. He thought that all in all he was a very lucky guy. Escaping monsters, ghosts and traps, seeing a reindeer (the girls had told him it was a moose, but he didn't believe that), finding such a rich variety of food and fending off a huge dog, and here he was with friends who admired him, and a wonderful nest to sleep in, what more could any raccoon hope for? After catching Randy's glance, a minute earlier, Rosie had sidled up to him and was now gazing thoughtfully over the lake with a dreamy look on her face. She seemed happy too he thought.

"Would you like to stay here with me?" he burst out suddenly.

She turned her head towards him, smiled and said, "I would", and then looked back over the lake which had lost all its sunset colours.

Black and white wavelets lapped at the rocks on the shore. A loon called its long, lonely cry from the lake and the frogs continued to sing their songs. The raccoon friends set off to explore the edge of the lake and the area around "their tree" some more. It turned out to be even better than they had thought. The hole in the tree had a south view, sheltered by pines, birches and poplars. There were seeds, berries, nuts and all the bounty of the lake and nearby farms to eat. They had each other for company and safety, had played together, fought together, liked and trusted each other. It would be nice to have a secure home without having to worry about people. Gramma and Poppa had been okay. They hadn't usually bothered Randy, but if Gramma couldn't share her garden, and Poppa used traps, well, obviously they were problems.

IN THEIR TREE

Randy snuggled up closer to Rosie and asked, "Is this home?"

Rosie turned a beaming face toward him and replied, "Our very first home!"

And so it was, that Randy and Rosie made the hole in that big old tree into a warm and safe nest. They were never bothered again by the farm dog, preferring to get their fresh eggs at the farm where Rosie's parents lived.

And one day, Rhonda left to visit some friends in the city, while Randy and Rosie were having a holiday by their favourite lake. She never moved back and later they learned that she liked the city life.

The end of Randy's tail never grew back. The tip had been bitten right off, but the next year he met a young raccoon with a similar kind of squared off end and learned that it had become the newest fashion among young males!

SOME INTERESTING FACTS ABOUT RACCOONS

1. Where do they live? Raccoons live almost every where; in marshes, prairies, forests, cities, people's attics and outbuildings, fields, trees, caves, or at the base of fence posts.

2. Could Randy have seen a reindeer? Although they don't hibernate, raccoons sleep for extended periods if the weather is very cold. Their natural territory is North America and northern South America, although they have been introduced into other countries. They do not live in the far north, so Randy's best chance of seeing a reindeer would be in a zoo!

3. They are active in daytime or at night, but are nocturnal foragers, which means that they look for their food at night.

4. What do they look like? They are often called "masked bandits", because of the black masklike patch over their eyes. Their tails are long and bushy with four to seven black rings. They normally weigh anywhere between four to thirty pounds depending on their diet, health and environment. There are different sizes and colours of raccoons in different countries. In Mexico, their coats are almost plain whitish in colour.

5. What does their poop look like? Since the raccoon is similar in size to a smallish dog, their poop is also

similar—and may contain seeds, berries and bits of shells or whatever they have eaten. It is very stinky and dangerous for humans to touch, as many raccoons have a kind of worm in their poop, which can cause sickness.

6. What do they eat? Raccoons eat almost everything, like us, which makes them omnivores. They like sweet foods best and are not very keen on sour things. Fruits, plants, seeds, flowers, frogs, worms and insects, mussels, crabs, snails, crayfish, nuts, vegetables, small animals and eggs are their basic diet. They collect food from water very often and then rub it which looks as though they are washing it. This is called dousing. They might douse some food that is near water, but they do not usually wash food before they eat it.

7. Who are their enemies? The most common enemy of raccoons is the dog, although raccoons can be vicious fighters, with very sharp teeth and claws. Bobcats, coyotes, bears, wolves, cougars and lynxes are also their natural predators and baby raccoons can be hunted by owls and eagles.

8. Are they smart? Raccoons are very intelligent animals with very good memories. They can figure out how to do complicated things very quickly and then remember them afterwards.

9. Are they good climbers? Raccoons are very good climbers and that is how they usually get away from predators. They can't climb on very smooth surfaces but could jump several feet across an area

such as from a tree to a roof. But one of the most interesting things about how raccoons climb, is that they can go down trees facing forwards, but they turn their hind paws backwards!

10. How long do they live? Raccoons do not live very long in the wild, usually no more than two or three years, although if they were healthy with a very good environment, they could live to be as old as fifteen. Born in the springtime, from two to five kits or cubs normally stay with their mothers until the autumn, when they go off to live on their own.

11. Do raccoons make good pets? No, raccoons are wild animals and can be quite vicious. As well, they are the most common carrier of rabies and their poop very often has roundworm in it that can cause many serious diseases. They may look like cuddly animals, but they are not.

12. What do raccoon tracks look like? Raccoon tracks look a lot like those of little human beings. Their paws on the front and back are like hands and feet with five digits each. The back paws are longer than the front ones, like our feet are, but our toes are much shorter than their hind digits. They do not have opposable thumbs like we do, but they have very dexterous and sensitive front paws that can do amazingly complicated tasks.

13. With fur coats on, how do they cool off? Raccoons have a dual cooling system, which means that they have two different ways to cool off. They sweat like we do

through pores in their skin and they also pant from their mouths like dogs do. If they are very hot, their tongues might drip.

14. How do instincts affect them? Although you might think that this question has to do with how stinky they are, it means what they do naturally without thinking, like breathing. Raccoons have very sharp hearing. They can hear earthworms digging in the earth and clams opening in the water. Loud noises can frighten them so badly that they are unable to move, or else, sometimes they pee without even knowing they are doing so. Not only do their ears work better than ours, but their front paws do as well. Their nails are longer and stronger than ours, which helps them dig and open small objects. When these paws get wet, the skin which is usually rather leathery, will soften and be able to feel extra well. Feeling, hearing and smelling are senses which we have too, but for raccoons these are developed more strongly, which helps them to detect danger.

15. Raccoons don't really have whiskers on their toes, do they? Yes, they do! And those whiskers which are called vibrissae are extremely sensitive. In fact, more than half of the information received by their brains is sent from those whiskers.

16. Raccoons don't really use toilets, do they? Yes, raccoons do use communal latrines. Because their noses work so well, and their poop is so stinky, they find places which all the raccoons in an area will use as a toilet.

17. Did Davy Crockett really wear a hat with a raccoon's tail on it? Actually, there were two Davy Crockett's in American history, whose stories put together make up the one we know, about the wild frontiersman who is said to have worn a "coonskin" cap with the tail hanging down. There is no proof that it is true, but raccoon fur has been used to make coats and hats for people for hundreds of years. Raccoon fur has two different layers. The top one which is longer and stronger is waterproof. The underneath layer is very soft and warm.

18. Are raccoons a kind of pig? No, they are not pigs, but the males are known as boars and the females are sows which are the words used for male and female pigs.

19. How many ways did you notice that people and raccoons are alike?